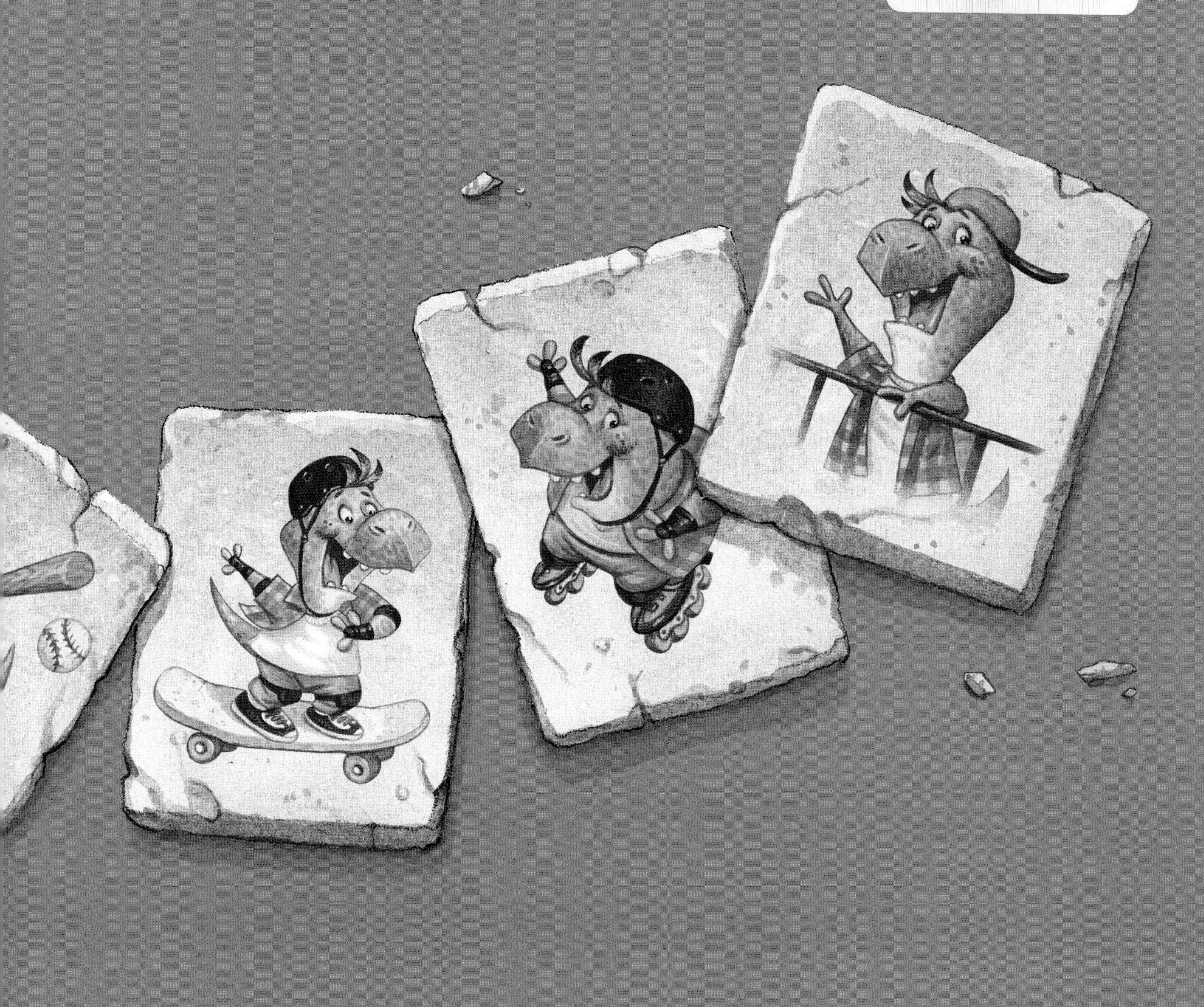

Are you ready?
Are you steady?
Is your first name Freddy?
Well, listen to me. . . .

RAPPY

the RAPTOR

To Tamar Mays

—D.G.

To Ava and Noah

—T.B.

 For information address HarperCollins Children's Books, a division of HarperCollins Publishers, 195 Broadway, New York, NY 10007.
www.harpercollinschildrens.com

Library of Congress Cataloging-in-Publication Data
Gutman, Dan.
Rappy the raptor / by Dan Gutman ; illustrated by Tim Bowers. — First edition.
pages cm
Summary: "Rappy the Raptor tells the story of how he became a rapping velociraptor, all in rhyme"— Provided by publisher.
ISBN 978-0-06-229180-6 (hardcover)
[1. Stories in rhyme. 2. Velociraptor—Fiction. 3. Dinosaurs—Fiction. 4. Rap (Music)—Fiction. 5. Medical care—Fiction.] I. Bowers, Tim, illustrator. II. Title.
PZ8.3.G9638Rap 2015 2014005875
[E]—dc23 CIP
AC

The artist used acrylic paint, using paintbrushes and a sponge on watercolor board, to create the illustrations for this book.
Typography by Rick Farley
15 16 17 18 19 SCP 10 9 8 7 6 5 4 3 2 1
❖
First Edition

RAPPY the RAPTOR

By Dan Gutman

Illustrated by Tim Bowers

HARPER
An Imprint of HarperCollins*Publishers*

I'm Rappy the Raptor
and I'd like to say,
I may not talk in the usual way.

I'm rhymin' and rappin'
all of the time.
I'm talkin' when I'm walking
and I'm rhymin' when I climb.

I'm rappin' at my school
and I'm rappin' with my peeps.
Sometimes they even tell me
that I'm rappin' in my sleep.

Now, how did it happen
that I started rappin'?
Well, here's my story
in all its glory!

I was born in a tree
back in Memphis, Tennessee.
My mom (that's Mappy)
and my dad (that's Pappy)
took one look at me
and got oh so happy!

When I popped from my egg,
hip-hoppin' on my leg,
I tried to fly
(and I don't know why),
but the next thing I knew,
I was falling from the sky!

I landed on a shed
and I smacked my head.
I turned all red.
I had to go to bed!

But here's the big surprise:
When I opened up my eyes,
I was feeling just fine,
and I was talking in rhyme!

I'm Rappy the Raptor
and I'd like to say,
I may not talk in the usual way.

I'm rappin' in the morning,
I'm rappin' at noon.
I'm rappin' in October
and I'm rappin' in June.

My parents freaked out;
they didn't know what to do.
Should they take me to the doctor?
Or take me to the zoo?

They rushed me to the hospital;
the ambulance was screaming.
The nurse gave me a Popsicle;
I thought that I was dreaming!

The doctors looked me in the eye
and looked me in the ear.
And I'm not ashamed to say
they even looked me in the rear.

Next they put me in a box
that took pictures of my guts.
It made a bunch of noises.
I thought I would go nuts!

They scanned my lung,
they poked my nose.
They scraped my tongue,
they yanked my toes.

But they couldn't figure out what happened.
Nobody knew why I was rappin'.

I'm Rappy the Raptor
and I'd like to say,
I may not talk in the usual way.
I'm rappin' in the morning,
I'm rappin' at noon.
I'm rappin' with the doctors.
I want to go home soon.

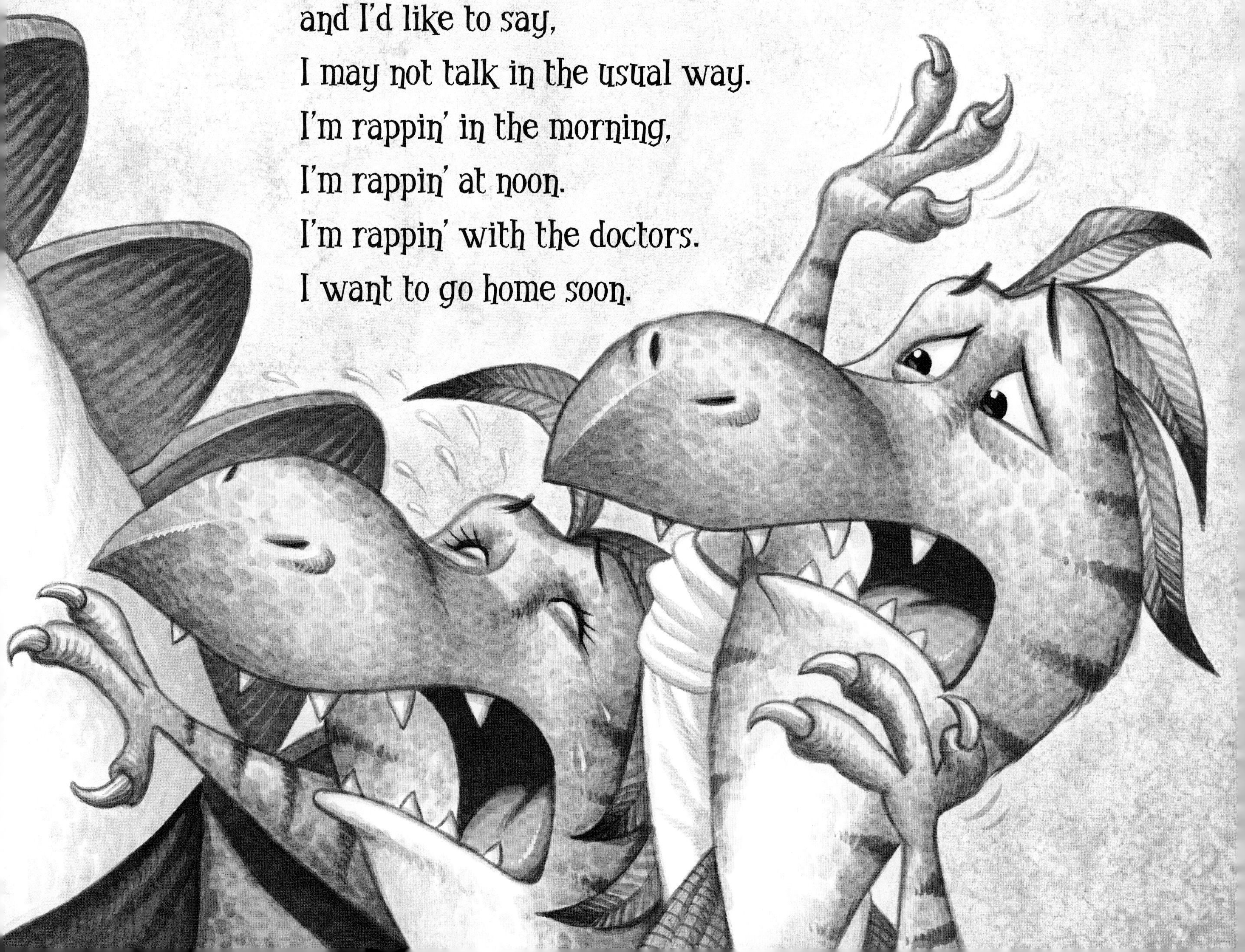

They took me to a lab—
hooked me up to weird machines.
They ran all kinds of tests
and watched computer screens.

They made me look at dots.
I had to pee in pots!
Some guy gave me a shot;
that didn't feel too hot!

After doing all those tests
they told me to get dressed.
I was expecting the worst.
I thought that I would burst.

The doctor stood up
and put down his coffee cup.
His name was Dr. Ted,
and this is what he said. . . .

"After much confusion,
we have come to our conclusion. . . .

"There's no need to be formal.

RAPPY'S PERFECTLY NORMAL!

"He's A-okay,
that's what we want to say.
Don't blame it on the fall.
He was *born* this way!"

Then the doctors started boppin'.
Their fingers started snappin'.
The nurses started hoppin',
and I started rappin'. . . .

I'm Rappy the Raptor
and I'd like to say,
I may not talk in the usual way.

I'm rhymin' and rappin'
all of the time.
I'm rappin' when I'm riding
and I'm rhymin' when I climb.

I'm rappin' in the playground,
I'm rappin' at the zoo.
I'm rappin' on the sidewalk
and now I'm rappin' with YOU!